D1361689

Why Buster Beasly Was Late for Lunch

BY TEDDY SLATER
PICTURES BY LAURA RANKIN

Silver Press

For Judy, Mitch, and especially Paul Magrowski.
—T.S.

For my parents, with love
—L.R.

Library of Congress Cataloging-in-Publication Data

Slater, Teddy.
Why Buster Beasly was late for lunch / by Teddy Slater; pictures by Laura Rankin.
p. cm.—(Is that so?)
Summary: Buster gives his mother several exaggerated excuses for being late for lunch. At intervals readers are given a variety of similar excuses from which to choose.
[1. Excuses—Fiction. 2. Literary recreations.]
I. Rankin, Laura, ill. II. Title. III. Series: Slater, Teddy. Is that so?
PZ7.S6294Wh 1991
[E]—dc20 90-38177
ISBN 0-671-70411-7 (LSB) ISBN 0-671-70415-X CIP
AC

Produced by Small Packages, Inc.

Published by Silver Press, a division of
Silver Burdett Press, Inc.
Simon & Shuster, Inc.
Prentice Hall Bldg., Englewood Cliffs, NJ 07632.

Printed in the United States of America.

10 9 8 7 6 5 4 3 2 1

Buster Beasly was late for lunch. And, boy, was his mom mad.
"I hope you have a *very* good excuse," said Mrs. Beasly.
"I do," said Buster. "I really, truly do.

"I was on my way home," he began, "when a great, big giant with a great, big club blocked my path. I told him I was late, but he wouldn't let me by."

"Is that so?" said Mrs. Beasly.

"Not really," said Buster.

What do you think really kept Buster from coming home?

Did a grouchy gorilla
carry him off to the jungle?

Did a mean green dragon
drag him into his cave?

Did the Sandman sing
him to sleep?

Or did his best friend Freddy
ask him to play baseball?

"I told Freddy I couldn't play with him, because I was already late for lunch," Buster explained. "But he had a brand-new baseball bat that he wanted me to try out. So I said, 'Okay, but we'd better make it fast.'

"Freddy wound up and threw me his fastest fast ball.
I swung the bat as hard as I could—and hit a home run!

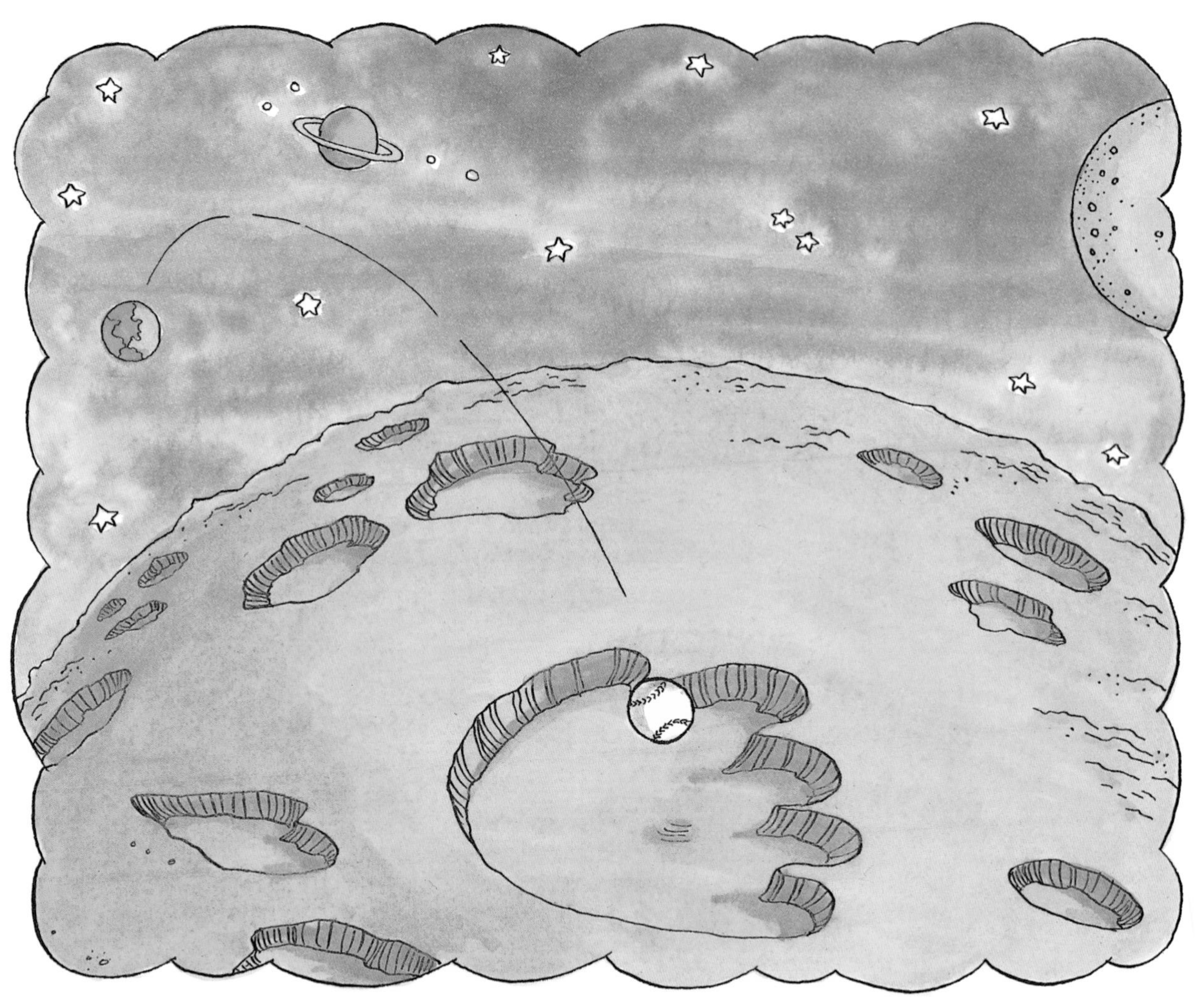

"The ball went whizzing past Freddy," Buster went on.
"And it came down a million miles away."
"Is that so?" said Mrs. Beasly.
"Not truly," said Buster.

How far do you think Buster truly hit the ball?

Did he hit it all the way
to the next town?

Did he hit it all the way
to New York City?

Did he hit it all the way
through Mrs. Wiggins' window?

Or did he hit it all the way
into outer space?

"After the ball broke Mrs. Wiggins' window,
I couldn't just leave," Buster told his mom.
"Even though I knew I was really late by then.

"So Freddy and I rang her doorbell and told her we were sorry. We said we would pay for the window out of our allowances. But she told us we didn't have to. 'If you really feel bad,' she said, 'you *could* mow my lawn for me. . . .'

"Well, Mom," Buster said, "we *did* feel bad— and her lawn sure needed mowing! The grass was so high, you could hardly see the house."

"Is that so?" said Mrs. Beasly.

"Not really," said Buster.

How high do you think the grass really was?

Was it exactly as high
as a dinosaur's eye,

almost as high as
a grasshopper's knee,

a little bit higher than
Buster's high-top sneakers,

or even higher than
a ripe field of corn?

"To tell the truth," said Buster, "that grass really wasn't much higher than the tops of my sneakers. But there was an awful lot of it. By the time we finished mowing, it was way past lunchtime.

"Mrs. Wiggins came out with a big pitcher of lemonade and a whole basket of sugar doughnuts—just for us. Freddy decided to stay. But I said I had to go, and I headed home—again.

"By then I wasn't only late," Buster told his mom, "I was really hungry! In fact, I was so hungry that my stomach started rumbling and grumbling. It was so loud that people came out of their houses to see what was going on."

"Is that so?" said Mrs. Beasly.

"Not truly," said Buster.

How loud do you think Buster's stomach truly was?

Was it as loud as
a tiger's terrible growl?

Was it a little louder than
a pussycat's purr?

Was it louder than a train
roaring down the track?

Or was it louder than
a big brass band
marching up the street?

"I guess my tummy did sound a lot like a pussycat's purr,"
Buster said. "Because suddenly I heard a really loud *Me-ow*!
I looked down, and there was this poor little kitten.
He was all alone and he was crying.

"I couldn't just leave him there," Buster said, opening his book bag and pulling out a little bundle of fur. "And that's why I'm late. I'm sorry, Mom. Really and truly, I am."

"Well, that's quite an excuse," said Mrs. Beasly. "I *was* very worried. But I'm glad you got home safely—both of you." Then she put a peanut butter and jelly sandwich on the table for Buster, and a saucer of milk on the floor for his kitten.